# DIPTYCH
# ROME-LONDON

# THE NEW DIRECTIONS

## *Bibelots*

KAY BOYLE
# THE CRAZY HUNTER

RONALD FIRBANK
# CAPRICE

HENRY MILLER
# A DEVIL IN PARADISE

EZRA POUND
# DIPTYCH ROME-LONDON

MURIEL SPARK
# THE DRIVER'S SEAT

DYLAN THOMAS
# EIGHT STORIES

TENNESSEE WILLIAMS
# THE ROMAN SPRING
# OF MRS. STONE

# EZRA POUND

# DIPTYCH ROME-LONDON

"HOMAGE TO SEXTUS PROPERTIUS"

"HUGH SELWYN MAUBERLEY"

With an Introduction by A. Walton Litz

A NEW DIRECTIONS

*Bibelot*

"Homage to Sextus Propertius" and "Hugh Selwyn Mauberley" are
also available in *Personae*, the collected shorter poems of Ezra
Pound, published by New Directions.

Manufactured in the United States of America
New Directions Books are printed on acid-free paper
First published as a New Directions Bibelot in 1994
Published simultaneously in Canada by Penguin Books Canada
Limited

Library of Congress Cataloging in Publication Data
Pound, Ezra, 1885–1972.
     [Homage to Sextus Propertius]
     Diptych Rome-London : Homage to Sextus Propertius, Hugh
Selwyn Mauberley / Ezra Pound ; with an introduction by
A. Walton Litz.
        p.   cm.
     ISBN 0–8112–1268–8 (alk. paper)
     1. Propertius, Sextus—Adaptations.   2. Elegiac poetry,
Latin—Adaptations.   I. Title.
PS3531.082A6   1994                                       93—50805
811'.52—dc20                                                   CIP

New Directions Books are published for James Laughlin
by New Directions Publishing Corporation,
80 Eighth Avenue, New York 10011

# Contents

## INTRODUCTION

*Diptych Rome-London* was first published in October 1958 in a sumptuous, limited edition of 200 numbered copies, each signed by the author. It was printed on a hand-press in Verona through the offices of two of Pound's friends and publishers, James Laughlin and Vanni Scheiwiller, with distribution in the United Kingdom by Faber & Faber and in the United States by New Directions. Pound had been released from St. Elizabeths Hospital in April 1958, so *Diptych* was in some ways a celebration of his return to Italy. It was also a much-needed reminder of his early achievements at a time when the controversy over the Bollingen Award for *The Pisan Cantos* was still fresh in the public mind.

Pound had always thought of *Homage to Sextus Propertius* and *Hugh Selwyn Mauberley* as a diptych, two facing panels that reflect the plight of the poet in a culture shaped by the First World War and the consequences of the Peace. In a note appended to *Mauberley* in *Personae: The Collected Poems* (1926) Pound stated that the "sequence is so distinctly a farewell to London that the reader who chooses to regard this as an exclusively American edition may as well omit it and turn at once to page 205 [the opening of *Homage to Sextus Propertius*]," and he once told a friend that *Mauberley* was "the poor man's Propertius." Writing to John Drummond in February 1932,

1

Pound wondered "how far the *Mauberley* is merely a translation of the *Homage to S. P.*, for such as couldn't understand the latter? An endeavour to communicate with a blockheaded epoch." Pound placed the *Homage* at the end of the 1926 *Personae: The Collected Poems* along with its date of composition (1917), a clear statement that he regarded this product of the darkest year of the war as the crown of his early poetic life. Of the two poems *Hugh Selwyn Mauberley* is more central to the development of modern poetry—a companion to Eliot's *The Waste Land* and Joyce's *Ulysses*—and it has always been the favorite of the general reader; but *Homage to Sextus Propertius* is often more admired by those who have followed Pound's early career through all its complex stages of development.

In 1914 Ezra Pound, the founder of Imagism and a key figure in the Vorticist movement, felt that he stood at the very center of the London literary world; he believed that he was a member of a small, elite group that could nevertheless have a profound impact on the course of social and literary history. By 1917 this faith was much diminished, and by 1920 Pound found himself a marginal figure, without power or influence in London. *Propertius* and *Mauberley* trace this decline, and provide a bittersweet background to Pound's ultimate decision to leave England for Paris and eventually Italy, where he labored on his long poem "containing history," *The Cantos,* for the next half-century.

In July 1916 Pound sent a typical pedagogical letter to the young Iris Barry, laying out an essential reading list for the would-be modern poet. In recommending Catullus and Propertius he remarked in passing: "if you CAN'T find *any* decent translations . . . I suppose I shall have to rig up something." The next year he did "rig up" Propertius, but the result was far from conventional translation. Instead he produced a true homage, one poet speaking to another, and learning from another, across the vast space that separated Propertius's Rome from Pound's London. In Pound's view, both poets were trying to find a place in a declining empire, with irony and satire as their prime defenses.

> Annalists will continue to record Roman
>             reputations,
> Celebrities from the Trans-Caucasus will
>                 belaud Roman celebrities
> And expound the distentions of Empire,
> But for something to read in normal
>             circumstances?
> For a few pages brought down from the
>             forked hill unsullied?

Like Propertius, Pound feels the pressure of imperial slogans and "official" literature, but in 1917 he can still respond with light-hearted verve and confidence. The contrast between the *Homage* and *Mauberley* is that between a poet who still looks to the future and a poet who can only speak bitterly, though often in beautiful elegiac cadences, of the past and the present.

When the *Homage* was first published many learned

readers who took it for an attempt at faithful translation mocked Pound's "blunders," and Pound's response—essentially a defense of his modernization of the poem—did not satisfy them. Pound does commit some obvious "howlers" in his reading of the Latin, but these in no way affect his overall intention, which is to turn Propertius into a mask for the contemporary poet. By highlighting what he took to be the hidden ironies of Propertius, the Latin poet's means for defending a private world, Pound made Propertius his contemporary. *Homage to Sextus Propertius* is an elegant example of the complicated, double transaction between past and present that Eliot would describe two years later in "Tradition and the Individual Talent."

The first part of *Hugh Selwyn Mauberley* was apparently written at great speed in late 1919. It begins with an ironic obituary for the aggressive, Odyssean poet "E. P.," who "For three years, out of key with his time," has sought "to resuscitate the dead art / Of poetry"; and then proceeds to a delicate, satiric examination of the immediate foreground and background of contemporary English poetry. The weaknesses of the Pre-Raphaelites and the decadent poets of the 'nineties are recorded with affectionate irony as the inevitable preludes to present-day vulgarity, and in two moving free-verse sections Pound mourns the loss of all those who died in the Great War.

> There died a myriad,
> And of the best, among them,

> For an old bitch gone in the teeth,
> For a botched civilization . . .

E. P. and his troublesome energies are buried under the weight of "official" mediocrity, and Part One closes with the elegiac "Envoi," a creative pastiche from a poetic tradition that has been all but forgotten in the contemporary world.

*Mauberley* was originally subtitled "Life and Contacts," but in the 1958 *Diptych* this was changed to "Contacts and Life," as if Pound wished to indicate clearly that Part One deals with the society which surrounded Hugh Selwyn Mauberley, while Part Two is a tracing of his abortive career. Part Two is an ironic reprise, in both style and theme, of Part One, and in it we are presented with the archetypal aesthete who cannot handle the pressures of a hostile environment. Mauberley is both the modern anti-hero in general and Pound's alter ego, a spectre that the poet must exorcise if he is to survive. Just as Joyce in writing "The Dead" justified his escape from Ireland through the portrait of his alter ego, Gabriel Conroy, so Pound sought to justify his departure from London by externalizing part of his earlier self in the figure of Hugh Selwyn Mauberley.

"Medallion," the last poem in the sequence, is a brilliant example of a style that Pound would leave behind him in writing *The Cantos*. It is certainly not, as some critics have claimed, an inferior and ironic companion to the "Envoi" that closes Part One. We do not have to choose between the two poems: one is a superb example of what can be done with the long sing-ing line, the other a chiselled triumph of sculptural form in words. But it is "Envoi," not "Medallion," that anticipates Pound's later poetry.

As T. S. Eliot noted in his Introduction to Pound's *Selected Poems* (1928), *Mauberley* is a great poem pre-cisely because it is so firmly rooted in the experiences of one man at one time in one place. It is a summation of Pound's early achievement as a poet, a memorial to the London years, and—like *The Waste Land*—a mas-ter document of literary modernism. But in its closed form *Mauberley* looks to the past, not the future, while the more open *Homage to Sextus Propertius,* in its counterpointing of past, present, and future, is a gate-way to *The Cantos.* The two poems do indeed form a diptych, and it is good to have them available once again in that form.

—A. Walton Litz

# HOMAGE
# TO  SEXTUS
# PROPERTIUS
## 1917


Orfeo
*"Quia pauper amavi."*

# I

Shades of Callimachus, Coan ghosts of Philetas
It is in your grove I would walk,
I who come first from the clear font
Bringing the Grecian orgies into Italy,
                    and the dance into Italy.
Who hath taught you so subtle a measure,
              in what hall have you heard it;
What foot beat out your time-bar,
         what water has mellowed your whistles?

Out-weariers of Apollo will, as we know, continue their
   Martian generalities,
    We have kept our erasers in order.
A new-fangled chariot follows the flower-hung horses;
A young Muse with young loves clustered about her
               ascends with me into the æther, . . .
And there is no high-road to the Muses.

Annalists will continue to record Roman reputations,
Celebrities from the Trans-Caucasus will belaud Roman
   celebrities
And expound the distentions of Empire,
But for something to read in normal circumstances?
For a few pages brought down from the forked hill
   unsullied?
I ask a wreath which will not crush my head.
             And there is no hurry about it;
I shall have, doubtless, a boom after my funeral,
Seeing that long standing increases all things
               regardless of quality.

And who would have known the towers
                        pulled down by a deal-wood horse;
Or of Achilles withstaying waters by Simois
Or of Hector spattering wheel-rims,
Or of Polydmantus, by Scamander, or Helenus and
   Deiphoibos?
Their door-yards would scarcely know them, or Paris.
Small talk O Ilion, and O Troad
                        twice taken by Oetian gods,
If Homer had not stated your case!


And I also among the later nephews of this city
                        shall have my dog's day,
With no stone upon my contemptible sepulchre;
My vote coming from the temple of Phoebus in Lycia,
   at Patara,
And in the meantime my songs will travel,
And the devirginated young ladies will enjoy them
                when they have got over the strangeness,
For Orpheus tamed the wild beasts—
                     and held up the Threician river;
And Cithaeron shook up the rocks by Thebes
   and danced them into a bulwark at his pleasure,
And you, O Polyphemus? Did harsh Galatea almost
Turn to your dripping horses, because of a tune, under
   Aetna?
We must look into the matter.
Bacchus and Apollo in favour of it,
There will be a crowd of young women doing homage to my
   palaver,
Though my house is not propped up by Taenarian
   columns from Laconia (associated with Neptune and
   Cerberus),

Though it is not stretched upon gilded beams:
My orchards do not lie level and wide
                    as the forests of Phaeacia,
                    the luxurious and Ionian,
Nor are my caverns stuffed stiff with a Marcian vintage,
My cellar does not date from Numa Pompilius,
Nor bristle with wine jars,
Nor is it equipped with a frigidaire patent;
Yet the companions of the Muses
            will keep their collective nose in my books,
And weary with historical data, they will turn to my
      dance tune.

Happy who are mentioned in my pamphlets,
        the songs shall be a fine tomb-stone over their beauty.
            But against this?
Neither expensive pyramids scraping the stars in their
      route,
Nor houses modelled upon that of Jove in East Elis,
Nor the monumental effigies of Mausolus,
                    are a complete elucidation of death.

Flame burns, rain sinks into the cracks
And they all go to rack ruin beneath the thud of the years.
Stands genius a deathless adornment,
            a name not to be worn out with the years.

I had been seen in the shade, recumbent on cushioned
  Helicon,
The water dripping from Bellerophon's horse,
Alba, your kings, and the realm your folk
                    have constructed with such industry
Shall be yawned out on my lyre—with such industry.
My little mouth shall gobble in such great fountains,
"Wherefrom father Ennius, sitting before I came, hath
  drunk."

I had rehearsed the Curian brothers, and made remarks
  on the Horatian javelin
(Near Q. H. Flaccus' book-stall).
"Of" royal Aemilia, drawn on the memorial raft,
"Of" the victorious delay of Fabius, and the left-handed
                    battle at Cannae,
Of lares fleeing the "Roman seat" . . .
                    I had sung of all these
And of Hannibal,
                and of Jove protected by geese.
And Phoebus looking upon me from the Castalian tree,
Said then "You idiot! What are you doing with that water:
Who has ordered a book about heroes?
                    You need, Propertius, not think
About acquiring that sort of a reputation.
        Soft fields must be worn by small wheels,
Your pamphlets will be thrown, thrown often into a chair
Where a girl waits alone for her lover;
        Why wrench your page out of its course?

No keel will sink with your genius
      Let another oar churn the water,
Another wheel, the arena; mid-crowd is as bad as mid-sea."
He had spoken, and pointed me a place with his plectrum:

     Orgies of vintages, an earthen image of Silenus
Strengthened with rushes, Tegaean Pan,
The small birds of the Cytherean mother,
     their Punic faces dyed in the Gorgon's lake;
Nine girls, from as many countrysides
     bearing her offerings in their unhardened hands,

Such my cohort and setting. And she bound ivy to his
   thyrsos;
Fitted song to the strings;
                Roses twined in her hands.
And one among them looked at me with face offended,
Calliope:
     "Content ever to move with white swans!
Nor will the noise of high horses lead you ever to battle;
Nor will the public criers ever have your name
                   in their classic horns,
Nor Mars shout you in the wood at Aeonia,
     Nor where Rome ruins German riches,
Nor where the Rhine flows with barbarous blood,
      and flood carries wounded Suevi.
Obviously crowned lovers at unknown doors,
Night dogs, the marks of a drunken scurry,
These are your images, and from you the sorcerizing
   of shut-in young ladies,
The wounding of austere men by chicane."
      Thus Mistress Calliope,
      Dabbling her hands in the fount, thus she
Stiffened our face with the backwash of Philetas the Coan.

Midnight, and a letter comes to me from our mistress:
    Telling me to come to Tibur:
                          *At* once!!
"Bright tips reach up from twin towers,
Anienan spring water falls into flat-spread pools."

What *is* to be done about it?
    Shall I entrust myself to entangled shadows,
Where bold hands may do violence to my person?

Yet if I postpone my obedience
                    because of this respectable terror,
I shall be prey to lamentations worse than a nocturnal
    assailant.
*And* I shall be in the wrong,
                  *and* it will last a twelve month,
For her hands have no kindness me-ward,


Nor is there anyone to whom lovers are not sacred at
    midnight
    And in the Via Sciro.
If any man would be a lover
               he may walk on the Scythian coast,
No barbarism would go to the extent of doing him harm,
The moon will carry his candle,
              the stars will point out the stumbles,
Cupid will carry lighted torches before him
                and keep mad dogs off his ankles.
Thus all roads are perfectly safe
                  and at any hour;

Who so indecorous as to shed the pure gore of a suitor?!
Cypris is his cicerone.
What if undertakers follow my track,
such a death is worth dying.
She would bring frankincense and wreaths to my tomb,
She would sit like an ornament on my pyre.

Gods' aid, let not my bones lie in a public location
With crowds too assiduous in their crossing of it;
For thus are tombs of lovers most desecrated.

May a woody and sequestered place cover me with its
foliage
Or may I inter beneath the hummock
of some as yet uncatalogued sand;
At any rate I shall not have my epitaph in a high road.

# IV

*Difference of Opinion With Lygdamus*

Tell me the truths which you hear of our constant
               young lady, Lygdamus,
And may the bought yoke of a mistress lie with
               equitable weight on your shoulders;
For I am swelled up with inane pleasurabilities
               and deceived by your reference
To things which you think I would like to believe.

No messenger should come wholly empty,
               and a slave should fear plausibilities;
Much conversation is as good as having a home.
Out with it, tell it to me, all of it, from the beginning,
I guzzle with outstretched ears.
Thus? She wept into uncombed hair,
                    And you saw it.
Vast waters flowed from her eyes?
                 You, you Lygdamus
Saw her stretched on her bed,—
             it was no glimpse in a mirror;
No gawds on her snowy hands, no orfevrerie,
Sad garment draped on her slender arms.
Her escritoires lay shut by the bed-feet.
Sadness hung over the house, and the desolated female
   attendants
Were desolated because she had told them her dreams.

She was veiled in the midst of that place,
Damp woolly handkerchiefs were stuffed into her
   undryable eyes,
And a querulous noise responded to our solicitous
   reprobations.
For which things you will get a reward from me,
              Lygdamus?
To say many things is equal to having a home.
And the other woman "has not enticed me
                    by her pretty manners,
She has caught me with herbaceous poison,
       she twiddles the spiked wheel of a rhombus,
She stews puffed frogs, snake's bones, the moulted feathers of
   screech owls,

She binds me with ravvles of shrouds.
             Black spiders spin in her bed!
Let her lovers snore at her in the morning!
           May the gout cramp up her feet!
Does he like me to sleep here alone,
         Lygdamus?
Will he say nasty things at my funeral?"

And you expect me to believe this
         after twelve months of discomfort?

# V

Now if ever it is time to cleanse Helicon;
        to lead Emathian horses afield,
And to name over the census of my chiefs in the Roman
    camp.
If I have not the faculty, "The bare attempt would be
    praiseworthy."
"In things of similar magnitude
                the mere will to act is sufficient."


The primitive ages sang Venus,
                the last sings of a tumult,
And I also will sing war when this matter of a girl is
    exhausted.
I with my beak hauled ashore would proceed in a more
    stately manner,
My Muse is eager to instruct me in a new gamut, or
    gambetto,
Up, up my soul, from your lowly cantilation,
                put on a timely vigour.


Oh august Pierides! Now for a large-mouthed product.
Thus:
"The Euphrates denies its protection to the Parthian and
              apologizes for Crassus,"
And "It is, I think, India which now gives necks to your
    triumph,"
And so forth, Augustus. "Virgin Arabia shakes in her
    inmost dwelling."
If any land shrink into a distant seacoast,
    it is a mere postponement of your domination.

And I shall follow the camp, I shall be duly celebrated
        for singing the affairs of your cavalry.
May the fates watch over my day.


2

Yet you ask on what account I write so many love-lyrics
And whence this soft book comes into my mouth.
Neither Calliope nor Apollo sung these things into my ear,
        My genius is no more than a girl.

If she with ivory fingers drive a tune through the lyre,
        We look at the process.
How easy the moving fingers; if hair is mussed on her
        forehead,
If she goes in a gleam of Cos, in a slither of dyed stuff,
There is a volume in the matter; if her eyelids sink into
        sleep,
There are new jobs for the author;
And if she plays with me with her shirt off,
        We shall construct many Iliads.
And whatever she does or says
        We shall spin long yarns out of nothing.

Thus much the fates have allotted me, and if, Maecenas,
I were able to lead heroes into armour, I would not,
Neither would I warble of Titans, nor of Ossa
                        spiked onto Olympus,
Nor of causeways over Pelion,
Nor of Thebes in its ancient respectability,
                nor of Homer's reputation in Pergamus,
Nor of Xerxes' two-barreled kingdom, nor of Remus and
        his royal family,
Nor of dignified Carthaginian characters,
Nor of Welsh mines and the profit Marus had out of them.

I should remember Caesar's affairs . . .

                             for a background,

Although Callimachus did without them,

                     and without Theseus,

Without an inferno, without Achilles attended of gods,

Without Ixion, and without the sons of Menoetius and
   the Argo ⸗ and without Jove's grave and the Titans.


And my ventricles do not palpitate to Caesarial *ore
   rotundos,*
Nor to the tune of the Phrygian fathers.
Sailor, of winds; a plowman, concerning his oxen;
Soldier, the enumeration of wounds; the sheepfeeder,
   of ewes;
We, in our narrow bed, turning aside from battles:
Each man where he can, wearing out the day in his manner.


3

It is noble to die of love, and honourable to remain

                        uncuckolded for a season.

And she speaks ill of light women,

                    and will not praise Homer

Because Helen's conduct is "unsuitable."

# VI

When, when, and whenever death closes our eyelids,
Moving naked over Acheron
Upon the one raft, victor and conquered together,
Marius and Jugurtha together,
                              one tangle of shadows.

Caesar plots against India,
Tigris and Euphrates shall, from now on, flow at his
    bidding,
Tibet shall be full of Roman policemen,
The Parthians shall get used to our statuary
                              and acquire a Roman religion;
One raft on the veiled flood of Acheron,
                Marius and Jugurtha together.

Nor at my funeral either will there be any long trail,
                    bearing ancestral lares and images;
No trumpets filled with my emptiness,
Nor shall it be on an Attalic bed;
            The perfumed cloths shall be absent.
A small plebeian procession.
                Enough, enough and in plenty
There will be three books at my obsequies
Which I take, my not unworthy gift, to Persephone.

You will follow the bare scarified breast
Nor will you be weary of calling my name, nor too weary
            To place the last kiss on my lips
When the Syrian onyx is broken.

          "He who is now vacant dust
          Was once the slave of one passion:"
Give that much inscription
          "Death why tardily come?"

You, sometimes, will lament a lost friend,
          For it is a custom:
This care for past men,

Since Adonis was gored in Idalia, and the Cytherean
Ran crying with out-spread hair,
          In vain, you call back the shade,
In vain, Cynthia. Vain call to unanswering shadow,
          Small talk comes from small bones.

## VII

Me happy, night, night full of brightness;
Oh couch made happy by my long delectations;
How many words talked out with abundant candles;
Struggles when the lights were taken away;
Now with bared breasts she wrestled against me,
            Tunic spread in delay;
And she then opening my eyelids fallen in sleep,
Her lips upon them; and it was her mouth saying:
    Sluggard!

In how many varied embraces, our changing arms,
Her kisses, how many, lingering on my lips.
"Turn not Venus into a blinded motion,
           Eyes are the guides of love,
Paris took Helen naked coming from the bed of Menelaus,
Endymion's naked body, bright bait for Diana,"
          —such at least is the story.

While our fates twine together, sate we our eyes with love;
For long night comes upon you
             and a day when no day returns.
Let the gods lay chains upon us
        so that no day shall unbind them.

Fool who would set a term to love's madness,
For the sun shall drive with black horses,
           earth shall bring wheat from barley,
The flood shall move toward the fountain
           Ere love know moderations,
           The fish shall swim in dry streams.
No, now while it may be, let not the fruit of life cease.

Dry wreaths drop their petals,
        their stalks are woven in baskets,
To-day we take the great breath of lovers,
        to-morrow fate shuts us in.

Though you give all your kisses
        you give but few.

Nor can I shift my pains to other,
        Hers will I be dead,
If she confer such nights upon me,
        long is my life, long in years,
If she give me many,
        God am I for the time.

## VIII

Jove, be merciful to that unfortunate woman
        Or an ornamental death will be held to your debit,
The time is come, the air heaves in torridity,
The dry earth pants against the canicular heat,
But this heat is not the root of the matter:
            She did not respect all the gods;
Such derelictions have destroyed other young ladies
    aforetime,
And what they swore in the cupboard
                    wind and wave scattered away.

Was Venus exacerbated by the existence of a comparable
    equal?
            Is the ornamental goddess full of envy?
Have you contempted Juno's Pelasgian temples,
            Have you denied Pallas good eyes?
Or is it my tongue that wrongs you
                with perpetual ascription of graces?
There comes, it seems, and at any rate
        through perils, (so many) and of a vexed life,
The gentler hour of an ultimate day.

Io mooed the first years with averted head,
            And now drinks Nile water like a god,
Ino in her young days fled pellmell out of Thebes,
            Andromeda was offered to a sea-serpent
                and respectably married to Perseus,
Callisto, disguised as a bear,
                wandered through the Arcadian prairies
                While a black veil was over her stars,

What if your fates are accelerated,
                    your quiet hour put forward,
You may find interment pleasing,

You will say that you succumbed to a danger identical,
                    charmingly identical, with Semele's,
And believe it, and she also will believe it,
                    being expert from experience,
And amid all the gloried and storied beauties of Maeonia
There shall be none in a better seat, not
                    one denying your prestige,

Now you may bear fate's stroke unperturbed,
Or Jove, harsh as he is, may turn aside your ultimate day.
Old lecher, let not Juno get wind of the matter,
Or perhaps Juno herself will go under,
                    If the young lady is taken?

There will be, in any case, a stir on Olympus.

## IX

1

The twisted rhombs ceased their clamour of
    accompaniment;
The scorched laurel lay in the fire-dust;
The moon still declined to descend out of heaven,

But the black ominous owl hoot was audible.

And one raft bears our fates
                on the veiled lake toward Avernus
Sails spread on cerulean waters, I would shed tears
        for two;
I shall live, if she continue in life,
        If she dies, I shall go with her.
Great Zeus, save the woman,
            or she will sit before your feet in a veil,
            and tell out the long list of her troubles.

2

Persephone and Dis, Dis, have mercy upon her,
There are enough women in hell,
                quite enough beautiful women,
Iope, and Tyro, and Pasiphae, and the formal girls of Achaia,
And out of Troad, and from the Campania,
Death has his tooth in the lot,
                Avernus lusts for the lot of them,
Beauty is not eternal, no man has perennial fortune,
Slow foot, or swift foot, death delays but for a season.

My light, light of my eyes,
                you are escaped from great peril,
Go back to Great Dian's dances bearing suitable gifts,
Pay up your vow of night watches
                    to Dian goddess of virgins,
And unto me also pay debt:
The ten nights of your company you have
                  promised me.

# X

Light, light of my eyes, at an exceeding late hour I was
    wandering,
And intoxicated,
                    and no servant was leading me,
And a minute crowd of small boys came from opposite,
                        I do not know what boys,
And I am afraid of numerical estimate,
And some of them shook little torches,
                        and others held onto arrows,
And the rest laid their chains upon me,
            and they were naked, the lot of them,
And one of the lot was given to lust.


"That incensed female has consigned him to our pleasure."
So spoke. And the noose was over my neck.
And another said "Get him plumb in the middle!
            Shove along there, shove along!"
And another broke in upon this:
                    "He thinks that we are not gods."
"And she has been waiting for the scoundrel,
                and in a new Sidonian night cap,
And with more than Arabian odours,
                    God knows where he has been.
She could scarcely keep her eyes open
                        enter that much for his bail.
                            Get along now!"

We were coming near to the house,
> and they gave another yank to my cloak,
And it was morning, and I wanted to see if she was
  alone, and resting,
And Cynthia was alone in her bed.
> > I was stupefied.
I had never seen her looking so beautiful,
> No, not when she was tunick'd in purple.


Such aspect was presented to me, me recently emerged
  from my visions,
You will observe that pure form has its value.


"You are a very early inspector of mistresses.
Do you think I have adopted your habits?"
> There were upon the bed no signs of a voluptuous
> > encounter,
> No signs of a second incumbent.


She continued:
> "No incubus has crushed his body against me,
> Though spirits are celebrated for adultery.
> And I am going to the temple of Vesta . . ."
> > > and so on.


Since that day I have had no pleasant nights.

# XI

The harsh acts of your levity!
                              Many and many.
I am hung here, a scare-crow for lovers.

**2**

Escape! There is, O Idiot, no escape,
    Flee if you like into Tanais,
                        desire will follow you thither,
Though you heave into the air upon the gilded Pegasean
    back,
Though you had the feathery sandals of Perseus
To lift you up through split air,
The high tracks of Hermes would not afford you shelter.

Amor stands upon you, Love drives upon lovers,
                          a heavy mass on free necks.

It is our eyes you flee, not the city,
You do nothing, you plot inane schemes against me,
Languidly you stretch out the snare
                  with which I am already familiar,

And yet again, and newly rumour strikes on my ears.

Rumours of you throughout the city,
                  and no good rumour among them.

"You should not believe hostile tongues.
            Beauty is slander's cock-shy.
All lovely women have known this."
            "Your glory is not outblotted by venom,
Phoebus our witness, your hands are unspotted."
A foreign lover brought down Helen's kingdom
            and she was led back, living, home;
The Cytherean brought low by Mars' lechery
            reigns in respectable heavens, . . .

Oh, oh, and enough of this,
            by dew-spread caverns,
The Muses clinging to the mossy ridges;
            to the ledge of the rocks:
Zeus' clever rapes, in the old days,
            combusted Semele's, of Io strayed.
Oh how the bird flew from Trojan rafters,
Ida has lain with a shepherd, she has slept between sheep.

            Even there, no escape
Not the Hyrcanian seaboard, not in seeking the shore
    of Eos.

All things are forgiven for one night of your games. . . .
Though you walk in the Via Sacra, with a peacock's tail
    for a fan.

# XII

Who, who will be the next man to entrust his girl to a
  friend?
Love interferes with fidelities;
The gods have brought shame on their relatives;
Each man wants the pomegranate for himself;
Amiable and harmonious people are pushed incontinent
  into duels,
A Trojan and adulterous person came to Menelaus under
  the rites of hospitium,
And there was a case in Colchis, Jason and that woman in
  Colchis;
And besides, Lynceus,
                    you were drunk.

Could you endure such promiscuity?
                  She was not renowned for fidelity;
But to jab a knife in my vitals, to have passed on a swig
  of poison,
Preferable, my dear boy, my dear Lynceus,
Comrade, comrade of my life, of my purse, of my person;
But in one bed, in one bed alone, my dear Lynceus,
          I deprecate your attendance;
I would ask a like boon of Jove.
And you write of Achelöus, who contended with Hercules,
You write of Adrastus' horses and the funeral rites
  of Achenor,

And you will not leave off imitating Aeschylus.
      Though you make a hash of Antimachus,
You think you are going to do Homer.
      And still a girl scorns the gods,
Of all these young women
      not one has enquired the cause of the world,
Nor the modus of lunar eclipses
      Nor whether there be any patch left of us
After we cross the infernal ripples,
      nor if the thunder fall from predestination;
Nor anything else of importance.

Upon the Actian marshes Virgil is Phoebus' chief of police,
      He can tabulate Caesar's great ships.
He thrills to Ilian arms,
      He shakes the Trojan weapons of Aeneas,
And casts stores on Lavinian beaches.
Make way, ye Roman authors,
      clear the street, O ye Greeks,
For a much larger Iliad is in the course of construction
(and to Imperial order)
Clear the streets, O ye Greeks!

And you also follow him "neath Phrygian pine shade:"
      Thyrsis and Daphnis upon whittled reeds,
And how ten sins can corrupt young maidens;
      Kids for a bribe and pressed udders,
Happy selling poor loves for cheap apples.

Tityrus might have sung the same vixen;
        Corydon tempted Alexis,
Head farmers do likewise, and lying weary amid their oats
They get praise from tolerant Hamadryads.
Go on, to Ascraeus' prescription, the ancient,
                respected, Wordsworthian:
"A flat field for rushes, grapes grow on the slope."


And behold me, small fortune left in my house.
Me, who had no general for a grandfather!
I shall triumph among young ladies of indeterminate
    character,
My talent acclaimed in their banquets,
        I shall be honoured with yesterday's wreaths.
And the god strikes to the marrow.


        Like a trained and performing tortoise,
I would make verse in your fashion, if she should
    command it,
With her husband asking a remission of sentence,
        And even this infamy would not attract
            numerous readers
Were there an erudite or violent passion,
For the nobleness of the populace brooks nothing below
    its own altitude.
One must have resonance, resonance and sonority . . .
    like a goose.

Varro sang Jason's expedition,
          Varro, of his great passion Leucadia,
There is song in the parchment; Catullus the highly
  indecorous,
Of Lesbia, known above Helen;
And in the dyed pages of Calvus,
          Calvus mourning Quintilia,
And but now Gallus had sung of Lycoris.
          Fair, fairest Lycoris—
The waters of Styx poured over the wound:
And now Propertius of Cynthia, taking his stand among
  these.

———————————————

# HUGH  SELWYN MAUBERLEY

## (Contacts and Life)

*"Vocat æstus in umbram"*
—Nemesianus, Ec. IV.

## E. P. ODE POUR L'ELECTION DE
## SON SEPULCHRE

For three years, out of key with his time,
He strove to resuscitate the dead art
Of poetry; to maintain "the sublime"
In the old sense. Wrong from the start—

No, hardly, but seeing he had been born
In a half savage country, out of date;
Bent resolutely on wringing lilies from the acorn;
Capaneus; trout for factitious bait;

Ἴδμεν γάρ τοι πάνθ', ὅσ' ἐνὶ Τροίῃ
Caught in the unstopped ear;
Giving the rocks small lee-way
The chopped seas held him, therefore, that year.

His true Penelope was Flaubert,
He fished by obstinate isles;
Observed the elegance of Circe's hair
Rather than the mottoes on sun-dials.

Unaffected by "the march of events,"
He passed from men's memory in *l'an trentuniesme*
*De son eage;* the case presents
No adjunct to the Muses' diadem.

## II

The age demanded an image
Of its accelerated grimace,
Something for the modern stage,
Not, at any rate, an Attic grace;

Not, not certainly, the obscure reveries
Of the inward gaze;
Better mendacities
Than the classics in paraphrase!

The "age demanded" chiefly a mould in plaster,
Made with no loss of time,
A prose kinema, not, not assuredly, alabaster
Or the "sculpture" of rhyme.

# III

The tea-rose tea-gown, etc.
Supplants the mousseline of Cos,
The pianola "replaces"
Sappho's barbitos.

Christ follows Dionysus,
Phallic and ambrosial
Made way for macerations;
Caliban casts out Ariel.

All things are a flowing,
Sage Heracleitus says;
But a tawdry cheapness
Shall outlast our days.

Even the Christian beauty
Defects—after Samothrace;
We see τὸ καλόν
Decreed in the market place.

Faun's flesh is not to us,
Nor the saint's vision.
We have the press for wafer;
Franchise for circumcision.

All men, in law, are equals.
Free of Pisistratus,
We choose a knave or an eunuch
To rule over us.

O bright Apollo,
τίν' ἄνδρα, τίν' ἥρωα, τίνα θεόν
What god, man, or hero
Shall I place a tin wreath upon!

# IV

These fought in any case,
and some believing,
            pro domo, in any case . . .

Some quick to arm,
some for adventure,
some from fear of weakness,
some from fear of censure,
some for love of slaughter, in imagination,
learning later . . .
some in fear, learning love of slaughter;

Died some, pro patria,
            non "dulce" non "et decor" . . .
walked eye-deep in hell
believing in old men's lies, then unbelieving
came home, home to a lie,
home to many deceits,
home to old lies and new infamy;
usury age-old and age-thick
and liars in public places.

Daring as never before, wastage as never before.
Young blood and high blood,
fair cheeks, and fine bodies;

fortitude as never before

frankness as never before,
disillusions as never told in the old days,
hysterias, trench confessions,
laughter out of dead bellies.

# V

There died a myriad,
And of the best, among them,
For an old bitch gone in the teeth,
For a botched civilization,

Charm, smiling at the good mouth,
Quick eyes gone under earth's lid,

For two gross of broken statues,
For a few thousand battered books.

# YEUX GLAUQUES

Gladstone was still respected,
When John Ruskin produced
"King's Treasuries"; Swinburne
And Rossetti still abused.

Fœtid Buchanan lifted up his voice
When that faun's head of hers
Became a pastime for
Painters and adulterers.

The Burne-Jones cartons
Have preserved her eyes;
Still, at the Tate, they teach
Cophetua to rhapsodize;

Thin like brook-water,
With a vacant gaze.
The English Rubaiyat was still-born
In those days.

The thin, clear gaze, the same
Still darts out faun-like from the half-ruin'd face,
Questing and passive. . . .
"Ah, poor Jenny's case" . . .

Bewildered that a world
Shows no surprise
At her last maquero's
Adulteries.

# "SIENA MI FE'; DISFECEMI MAREMMA"

Among the pickled fœtuses and bottled bones,
Engaged in perfecting the catalogue,
I found the last scion of the
Senatorial families of Strasbourg, Monsieur Verog.

For two hours he talked of Galliffet;
Of Dowson; of the Rhymers' Club;
Told me how Johnson (Lionel) died
By falling from a high stool in a pub . . .

But showed no trace of alcohol
At the autopsy, privately performed—
Tissue preserved—the pure mind
Arose toward Newman as the whiskey warmed.

Dowson found harlots cheaper than hotels;
Headlam for uplift; Image impartially imbued
With raptures for Bacchus, Terpsichore and the Church.
So spoke the author of "The Dorian Mood,"

M. Verog, out of step with the decade,
Detached from his contemporaries,
Neglected by the young,
Because of these reveries.

# BRENNBAUM

The sky-like limpid eyes,
The circular infant's face,
The stiffness from spats to collar
Never relaxing into grace;

The heavy memories of Horeb, Sinai and the forty years,
Showed only when the daylight fell
Level across the face
Of Brennbaum "The Impeccable."

# MR. NIXON

In the cream gilded cabin of his steam yacht
Mr. Nixon advised me kindly, to advance with fewer
Dangers of delay. "Consider
      Carefully the reviewer.

I was as poor as you are;
When I began I got, of course,
Advance on royalties, fifty at first," said Mr. Nixon,
"Follow me, and take a column,
Even if you have to work free.

Butter reviewers. From fifty to three hundred
I rose in eighteen months;
The hardest nut I had to crack
Was Dr. Dundas.

I never mentioned a man but with the view
Of selling my own works.
The tip's a good one, as for literature
It gives no man a sinecure.

And no one knows, at sight, a masterpiece.
And give up verse, my boy,
There's nothing in it."

.  .  .  .  .  .  .  .  .  .  .  .  .  .

Likewise a friend of Blougram's once advised me:
Don't kick against the pricks,
Accept opinion. The "Nineties" tried your game
And died, there's nothing in it.

# X

Beneath the sagging roof
The stylist has taken shelter,
Unpaid, uncelebrated,
At last from the world's welter

Nature receives him;
With a placid and uneducated mistress
He exercises his talents
And the soil meets his distress.

The haven from sophistications and contentions
Leaks through its thatch;
He offers succulent cooking;
The door has a creaking latch.

# XI

"Conservatrix of Milésien"
Habits of mind and feeling,
Possibly. But in Ealing
With the most bank-clerkly of Englishmen?

No, "Milesian" is an exaggeration.
No instinct has survived in her
Older than those her grandmother
Told her would fit her station.

## XII

"Daphne with her thighs in bark
Stretches toward me her leafy hands,"—
Subjectively. In the stuffed-satin drawing-room
I await The Lady Valentine's commands,

Knowing my coat has never been
Of precisely the fashion
To stimulate, in her,
A durable passion;

Doubtful, somewhat, of the value
Of well-gowned approbation
Of literary effort,
But never of The Lady Valentine's vocation:

Poetry, her border of ideas,
The edge, uncertain, but a means of blending
With other strata
Where the lower and higher have ending;

A hook to catch the Lady Jane's attention,
A modulation toward the theatre,
Also, in the case of revolution,
A possible friend and comforter.

.   .   .   .   .   .   .   .   .   .   .   .   .

Conduct, on the other hand, the soul
"Which the highest cultures have nourished"
To Fleet St. where
Dr. Johnson flourished;

Beside this thoroughfare
The sale of half-hose has
Long since superseded the cultivation
Of Pierian roses.

49

## ENVOI (1919)

*Go, dumb-born book,*
*Tell her that sang me once that song of Lawes:*
*Hadst thou but song*
*As thou hast subjects known,*
*Then were there cause in thee that should condone*
*Even my faults that heavy upon me lie,*
*And build her glories their longevity.*

*Tell her that sheds*
*Such treasure in the air,*
*Recking naught else but that her graces give*
*Life to the moment,*
*I would bid them live*
*As roses might, in magic amber laid,*
*Red overwrought with orange and all made*
*One substance and one colour*
*Braving time.*

*Tell her that goes*
*With song upon her lips*
*But sings not out the song, nor knows*
*The maker of it, some other mouth,*
*May be as fair as hers,*
*Might, in new ages, gain her worshippers,*
*When our two dusts with Waller's shall be laid,*
*Siftings on siftings in oblivion,*
*Till change hath broken down*
*All things save Beauty alone.*

# MAUBERLEY

## 1920

*"Vacuos exercet in aera morsus."*

## I

Turned from the "eau-forte
Par Jacquemart"
To the strait head
Of Messalina:

"His true Penelope
Was Flaubert,"
And his tool
The engraver's.

Firmness,
Not the full smile,
His art, but an art
In profile;

Colourless
Pier Francesca,
Pisanello lacking the skill
To forge Achaia.

## II

*"Qu'est ce qu'ils savent de l'amour, et qu'est ce qu'ils peuvent comprendre?*

*S'ils ne comprennent pas la poésie, s'ils ne sentent pas la musique, qu'est ce qu'ils peuvent comprendre de cette passion en comparaison avec laquelle la rose est grossière et le parfum des violettes un tonnerre?"*

—Caid Ali

For three years, diabolus in the scale,
He drank ambrosia,
All passes, ANANGKE prevails,
Came end, at last, to that Arcadia.

He had moved amid her phantasmagoria,
Amid her galaxies,
NUKTOS AGALMA

. . . . . . .
Drifted . . . drifted precipitate,
Asking time to be rid of . . .
Of his bewilderment; to designate
His new found orchid. . . .

To be certain . . . certain . . .
(Amid ærial flowers) . . . time for arrangements—
Drifted on
To the final estrangement;

Unable in the supervening blankness
To sift TO AGATHON from the chaff
Until he found his sieve . . .
Ultimately, his seismograph:

—Given that is his "fundamental passion,"
This urge to convey the relation
Of eye-lid and cheek-bone
By verbal manifestation;

To present the series
Of curious heads in medallion—

He had passed, inconscient, full gaze,
The wide-banded irides
And botticellian sprays implied
In their diastasis;

Which anæsthesis, noted a year late,
And weighed, revealed his great affect,
(Orchid), mandate
Of Eros, a retrospect.

    . . . . .
Mouths biting empty air,
The still stone dogs,
Caught in metamorphosis, were
Left him as epilogues.

# "THE AGE DEMANDED"

Vide Poem II. Page 186

For this agility chance found
Him of all men, unfit
As the red-beaked steeds of
The Cytheræan for a chain bit.

The glow of porcelain
Brought no reforming sense
To his perception
Of the social inconsequence.

Thus, if her colour
Came against his gaze,
Tempered as if
It were through a perfect glaze

He made no immediate application
Of this to relation of the state
To the individual, the month was more temperate
Because this beauty had been.

       The coral isle, the lion-coloured sand
       Burst in upon the porcelain revery:
       Impetuous troubling
       Of his imagery.

Mildness, amid the neo-Nietzschean clatter,
His sense of graduations,
Quite out of place amid
Resistance to current exacerbations,

Invitation, mere invitation to perceptivity
Gradually led him to the isolation
Which these presents place
Under a more tolerant, perhaps, examination.


By constant elimination
The manifest universe
Yielded an armour
Against utter consternation,


A Minoan undulation,
Seen, we admit, amid ambrosial circumstances
Strengthened him against
The discouraging doctrine of chances,


And his desire for survival,
Faint in the most strenuous moods,
Became an Olympian *apathein*
In the presence of selected perceptions.


A pale gold, in the aforesaid pattern,
The unexpected palms
Destroying, certainly, the artist's urge,
Left him delighted with the imaginary
Audition of the phantasmal sea-surge,


Incapable of the least utterance or composition,
Emendation, conservation of the "better tradition,"
Refinement of medium, elimination of superfluities,
August attraction or concentration.

Nothing, in brief, but maudlin confession,
Irresponse to human aggression,
Amid the precipitation, down-float
Of insubstantial manna,
Lifting the faint susurrus
Of his subjective hosannah.

Ultimate affronts to
Human redundancies;

Non-esteem of self-styled "his betters"
Leading, as he well knew,
To his final
Exclusion from the world of letters.

**IV**


Scattered Moluccas
Not knowing, day to day,
The first day's end, in the next noon;
The placid water
Unbroken by the Simoon;

Thick foliage
Placid beneath warm suns,
Tawn fore-shores
Washed in the cobalt of oblivions;

Or through dawn-mist
The grey and rose
Of the juridical
Flamingoes;

A consciousness disjunct,
Being but this overblotted
Series
Of intermittences;

Coracle of Pacific voyages,
The unforecasted beach;
Then on an oar
Read this:

"I was
And I no more exist;
Here drifted
An hedonist."

# MEDALLION

Luini in porcelain!
The grand piano
Utters a profane
Protest with her clear soprano.

The sleek head emerges
From the gold-yellow frock
As Anadyomene in the opening
Pages of Reinach.

Honey-red, closing the face-oval,
A basket-work of braids which seem as if they were
Spun in King Minos' hall
From metal, or intractable amber;

The face-oval beneath the glaze,
Bright in its suave bounding-line, as,
Beneath half-watt rays,
The eyes turn topaz.